Place
photo
here

Bunny woke early this morning,
shaking the dreams from her head...

"This is my favorite day of the year.
Today is my birthday!" Bunny said.

The family came in and said with a grin,
"I know what we should do.
We should have a *birthday party*,
a party just for you."

5

Bunny made a list of friends,
inviting them all to come...

So they came with gifts,
played silly games,
and everyone had lots of fun.

When it was time for the birthday cake, everyone started to shout...

"Take a deep breath,
make a big wish,
and blow all the candles out!"

"I could wish to be an astronaut
in a rocket ship to Mars."

"Or maybe I'll wish to have a pony,
out on my beautiful farm.
She could run in the fields all day long,
and at night she would sleep in my barn."

12

"I might even wish to be an explorer,
who travels to lands untold.
I could discover hidden mines,
brimming with silver and gold."

"But what if the wish that I did choose,
was to be a big movie star?"

"To be a
veterinarian,
is one wish that I
could pick."

"I would heal little kittens,
and great big dogs,
or anything else that was sick."

After blowing really hard,
all the candles went out ...

as everyone danced about!

Nicholas

"I wished to be just where I am,
right here with all of you.
And when I opened up my eyes,
I saw it had come true."

"And in that wish I also wished,
just to be myself,
not to be an astronaut,
or a movie star with wealth."

"Because you see,
all of these wishes,
could still come true in time.
But for today I have to say,
I like being *Me* just fine!"

*Wishing you many
more birthdays!*
xo xo xo

27